SPLITONIO
AND HIS BORING SCHOOLWORK

WRITTEN BY RILEY JACOB BRACEY

ILLUSTRATIONS BY ANGELA LATHAM

Splitonio and His Boring Schoolwork

Copyright © 2020 Riley Jacob Bracey

Cover Art and Interior Illustrations Copyright © 2020 Angela Latham Designs

To request permissions, contact the publisher at info@urbaneenterprises.com.

ISBN: 978-0-578-71009-9

Library of Congress Control Number: 2020910788

Author: Riley Jacob Bracey

Illustrated and Designed by Angela Latham Designs

Edited by GiGi & Grannie

Published by Urbane Enterprises LLC: Madison, Mississippi

Printed in the United States of America

This book belongs to

_____

Splitonio never did any of his schoolwork.

All he wanted to do was play and swim at the waterin
hole with the other Spinosauruses.

One day, his school had a Schoolwork
Show-and-Tell Night.

His parents were looking for his work, but couldn't
find anything on the wall with his name on it.

His teacher, Mrs. Alvarez, who was a big Alvarezsaurus, told Splitonio's parents...

His parents were so angry that they scolded him!

"You will no longer be able to go to the watering hole to play until you put forth more effort!"

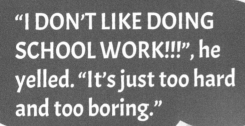

"I DON'T LIKE DOING SCHOOL WORK!!!", he yelled. "It's just too hard and too boring."

Splitonio was furious!

As he pouted and stomped away, he saw his classmat
Rexy the T-Rex.

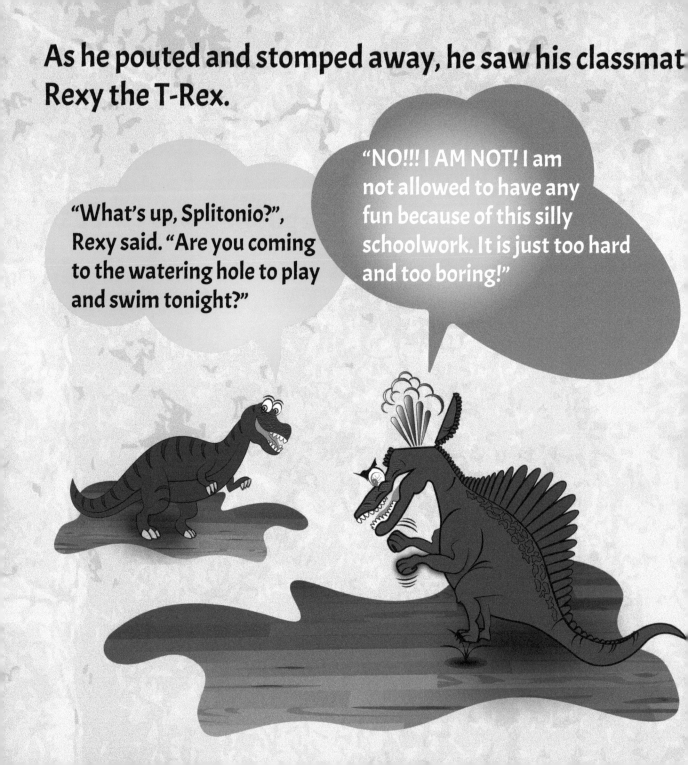

exy walked up to Splitonio.

exy explained to him that doing schoolwork was
ool, and allows you to learn and have great new ideas.

Splitonio looked at Rexy and smiled.

Splitonio replied with a sneaky grin on his face. "YOU can do all of my schoolwork for me, and then I will be able to go to the watering hole to swim and play whenever I want!"

Rexy looked at his friend
and frowned with sadness.

"I can't believe you are asking me
to do your schoolwork for you", h[e]
replied. "That is cheating!"

Splitonio could not believe his ears!

Rexy replied, "Don't worry about it Splitonio. I will help you with your work, so it won't be so hard and so boring. We can make fun games with our vocabulary words and math problems, design cool science experiments, and create awesome art projects with our pencils and crayons. Maybe we can also find you a tutor."

plitonio was so excited that his best friend Rexy was
oing to help him with his schoolwork and make it fun!

fter all, he did not want to be a cheater, and he really
vanted to swim and play at the watering hole with all
f the other dinosaurs.

A few weeks later, Splitonio started to enjoy his schoolwork, and was able to do it all on his own.

After seeing his great work on display at the next Schoolwork Show-and-Tell Night, his parents gave him a high five and allowed him to go to the watering hole.

They were so proud of his progress!

After learning that he was no longer on punishment, Splitonio invited Rexy to go to the watering hole with him.

He also gave him a big hug, and thanked him for encouraging him and being the BEST FRIEND EVER!

About the Author

A self-proclaimed "Dino Expert," 7-year old Riley Jacob Bracey dreamed of becoming an author after attending a live book reading of his favorite author, Dav Pilkey. The 2nd grader from Mississippi then put his pencil to paper, and his dreams became reality with the creation of his first book, "Splitonio and His Boring Schoolwork." In his spare time, Riley enjoys swimming, playing video games, basketball, football, and baseball. Prior to COVID-19, he also loved going to school and making new friends!

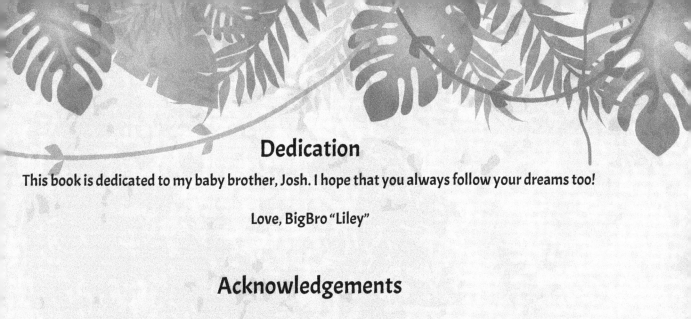

Dedication

This book is dedicated to my baby brother, Josh. I hope that you always follow your dreams too!

Love, BigBro "Liley"

Acknowledgements

To My Mom and Dad

Thank you Mom and Dad for allowing me to follow my dreams of becoming an author.

To Family and Friends

Special shout out to my Nana Shannon for helping me every step of the way, my GiGi and Grannie for being my editors, and the rest of my family for always supporting me in whatever I do.

Huge thanks to Ms. Angie for being such a patient illustrator and bringing my characters to life!

In Loving Memory of Uncle GP (Gerald Peyton)
If we had more teachers, coaches, and uncles like you, the world would be a much better place!

Love always, Riley J.

CPSIA information can be obtained
at www.ICGtesting.com
Printed in the USA
BVHW051359020920
587905BV00008B/152